Pride & Preju-STITCH

30 JANE AUSTEN—INSPIRED CROSS-STITCH BOOKMARKS

JANE AUSTEN

EDITED BY DOVER PUBLICATIONS

DOVER PUBLICATIONS

GARDEN CITY, NEW YORK

Pride and Preju-stitch: 30 Jane Austen–Inspired Cross-Stitch Bookmarks
is a new work, first published by Dover Publications in 2025.

ISBN-13: 978-0-486-85519-6
ISBN-10: 0-486-85519-8

Publisher: Betina Cochran
Acquisitions Editor: Allyson D'Antonio
Managing Editorial Supervisor: Susan Rattiner
Senior Production Editor: Michael Croland
Cover Designer: Peter Donahue
Creative Manager and Interior Designer: Marie Zaczkiewicz
Production: Pam Weston, Tammi McKenna, Ayse Yilmaz

Printed in China
85519801 2025
www.doverpublications.com

Contents

First Time Stitching?

How to Read a Cross-Stitch Chart

Cross-stitch charts are a guide for what colors to use and where they should go. In this book, all colors use DMC color codes.

The line numbers help you remember where you are.

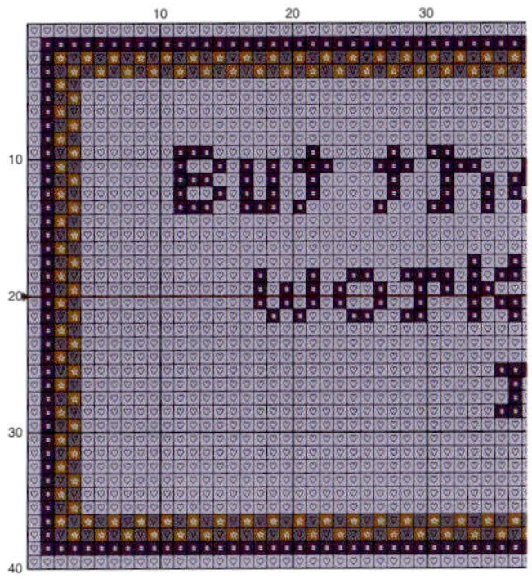

The arrows on the sides of the pattern designate the center of the chart.

Symbol	Number	Color Name
♡	26	Lavender White
▽	28	Lavender Gray
=	550	Passionflower
☆	782	Wicker

The table next to each chart shows you the symbol blocks and colors you will need for the project.

Every square in the chart is a single cross-stitch.

The Fabric

There are many different types of fabric for cross-stitch, but most stitchers use Aida cloth. The different Aida sizes will alter the measurements of the final design. Our patterns were designed with Aida 14 cloth in mind but will work on any fabric.

	Inches	Centimeters
Aida 14	7.14 x 2.57	18.14 x 6.53
Aida 16	6.25 x 2.25	15.88 x 5.72
Aida 18	5.56 x 2	14.11 x 5.08
Aida 20	5 x 1.8	12.7 x 4.57

Floss

This book uses DMC floss, and DMC numbers are listed for each project. Most DMC floss comes in six strands of cotton thread twisted together. For this project, you can use either two or three individual strands at a time.

Prepare the Hoop

For these projects, you may or may not wish to use a hoop. If you do use a hoop, loosen the outer screw and separate the two rings. Take your fabric and place it between the two loops, trying to center the fabric in the rings. Press down on the outer ring and tighten the screws until you have your desired tension.

The Needle

Cross-stitch needles traditionally have larger eyes than sewing needles, allowing you to use more strands of thread. The size of your needle will depend on the fabric used. Consult the chart below to find the proper needle size.

Aida Size	Needle Size
Aida 14	Size 24
Aida 16	Size 26
Aida 18	Size 28

Stitching Basics

Cross-stitches are done to create an *X* shape. You can stitch either from left to right or from right to left. When you start a project—or a new color/thread—start from the back of the fabric and bring your needle up through a front hole. Leave a bit of thread at the back so your stitches don't come undone.

Finishing

Keep stitching until you either run out of thread or finish the stitches in the pattern. Bring your thread to the back side of the project, and thread it under a few completed stitches to secure the thread. Then trim the excess.

Time to Stitch!

Pride & Preju-STITCH

Sense and Sensibility

Sense and Sensibility

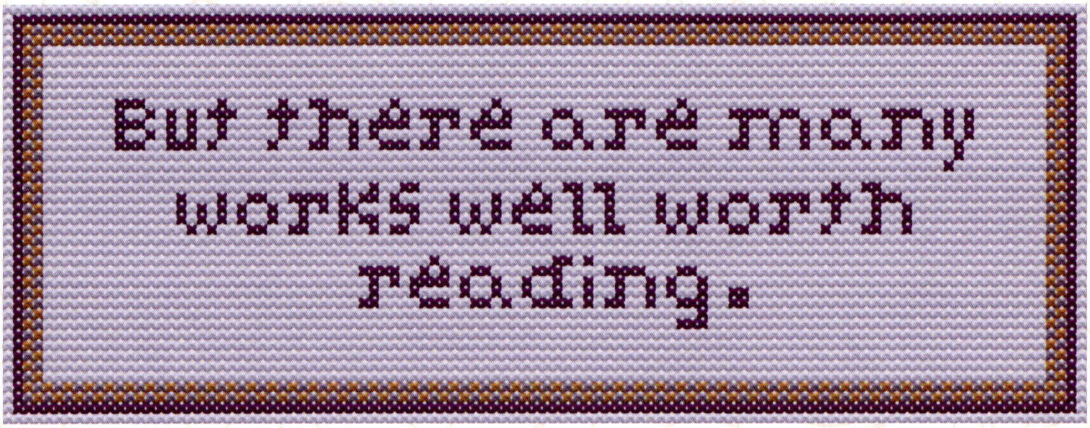

Symbol	Number	Color Name
♡	26	Lavender White
▽	28	Lavender Gray
=	550	Passionflower
☆	782	Wicker

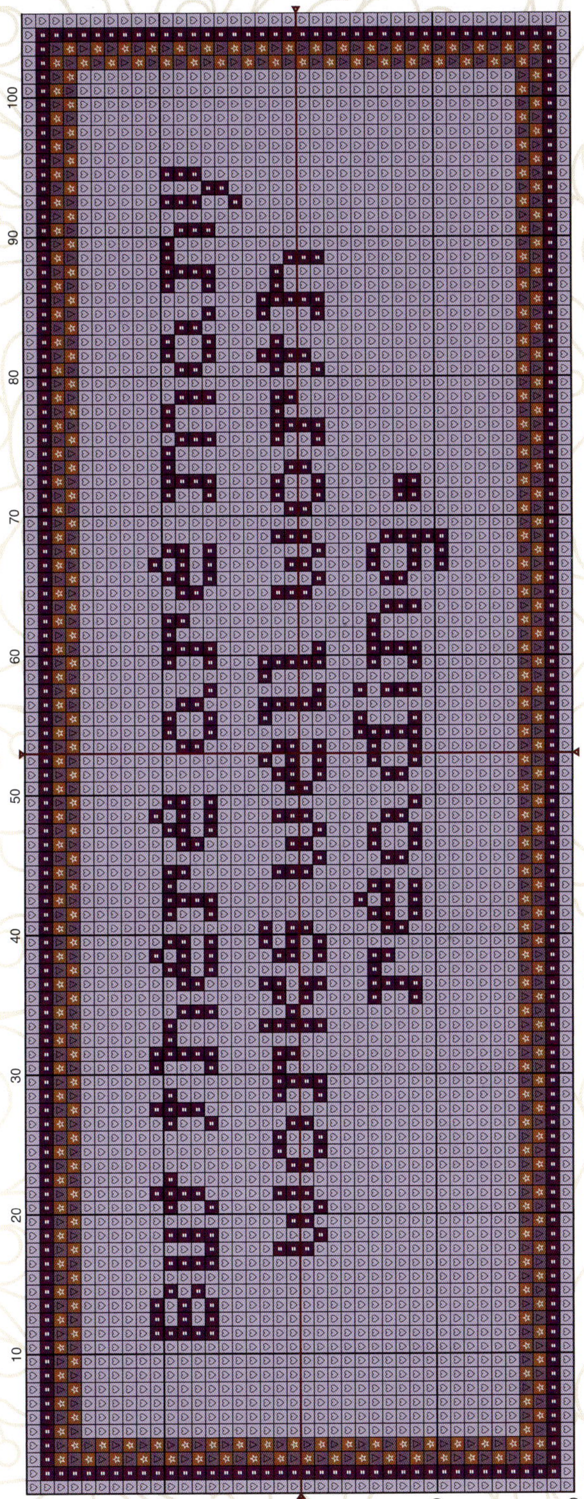

Sense and Sensibility

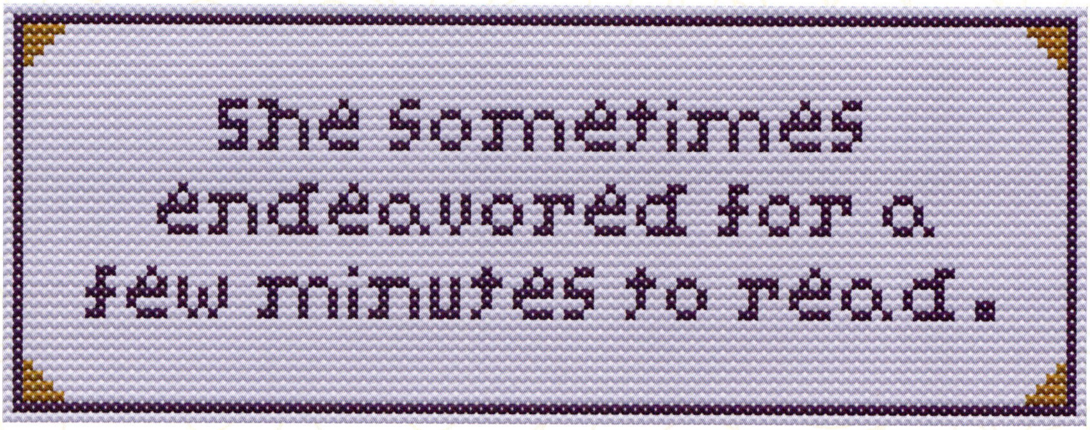

Symbol	Number	Color Name
♡	26	Lavender White
=	550	Passionflower
☆	782	Wicker

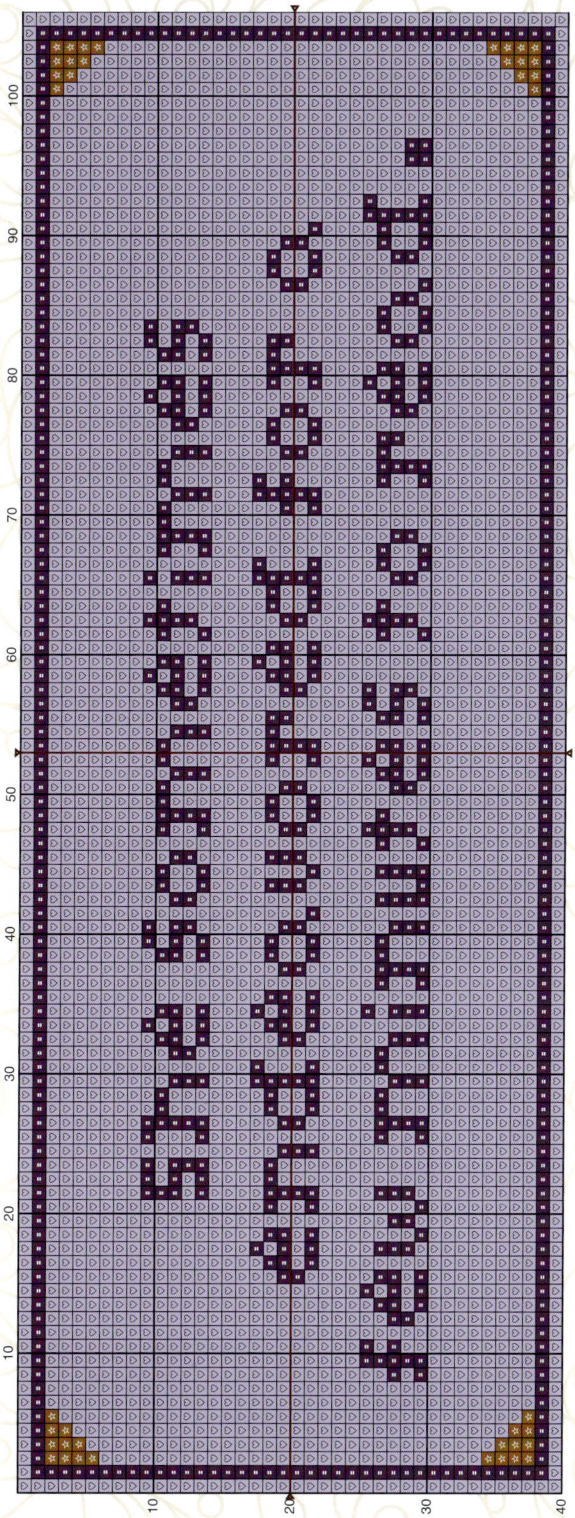

Sense and Sensibility

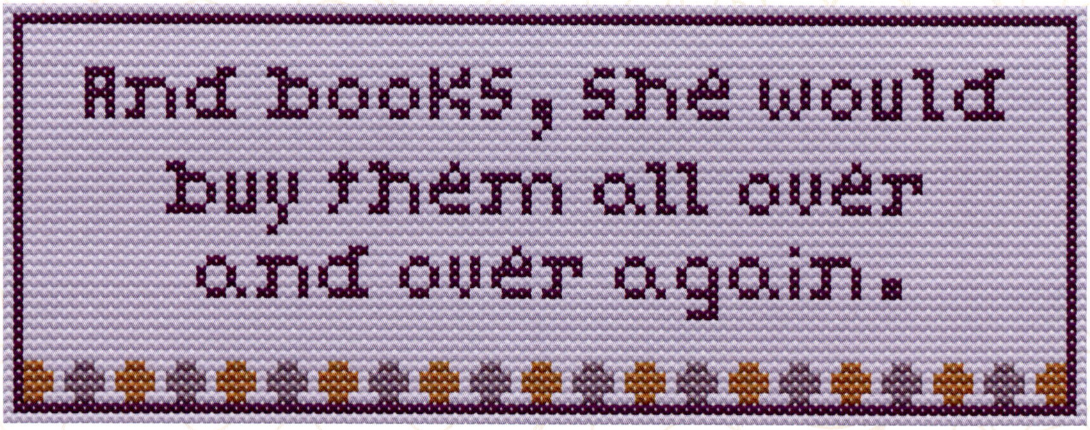

Symbol	Number	Color Name
♡	26	Lavender White
▽	28	Lavender Gray
=	550	Passionflower
☆	782	Wicker

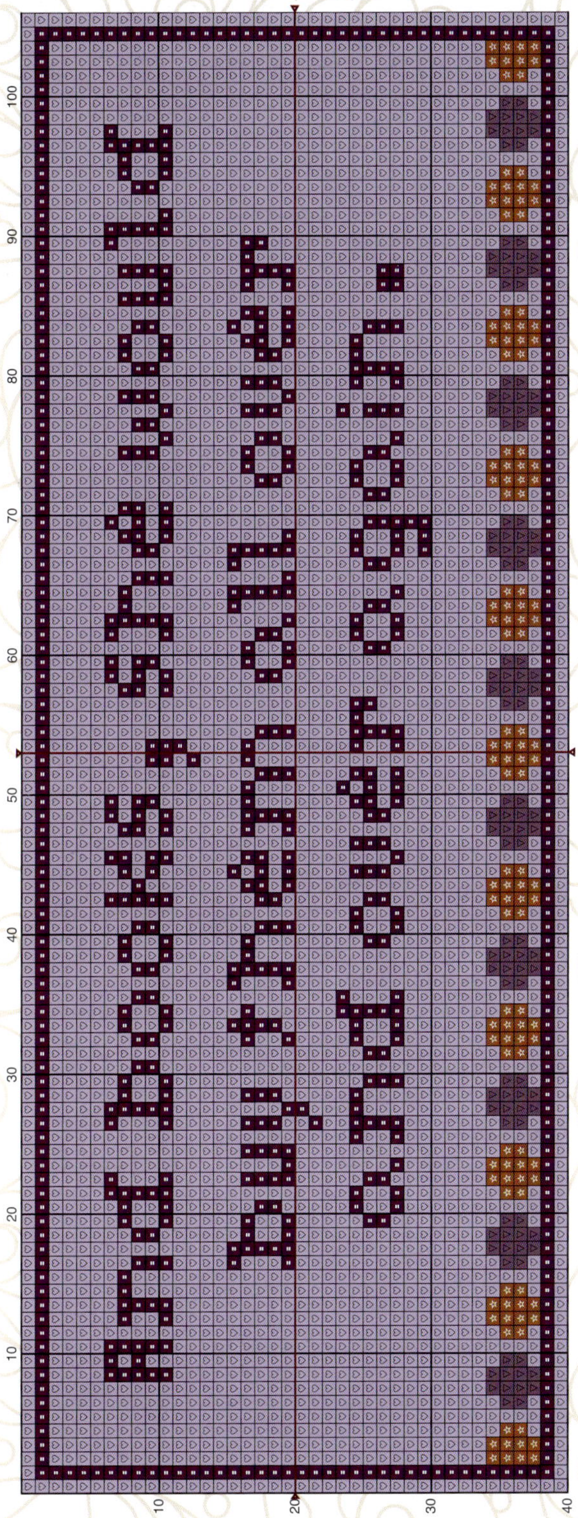

Sense and Sensibility

Symbol	Number	Color Name
♡	26	Lavender White
▽	28	Lavender Gray
=	550	Passionflower

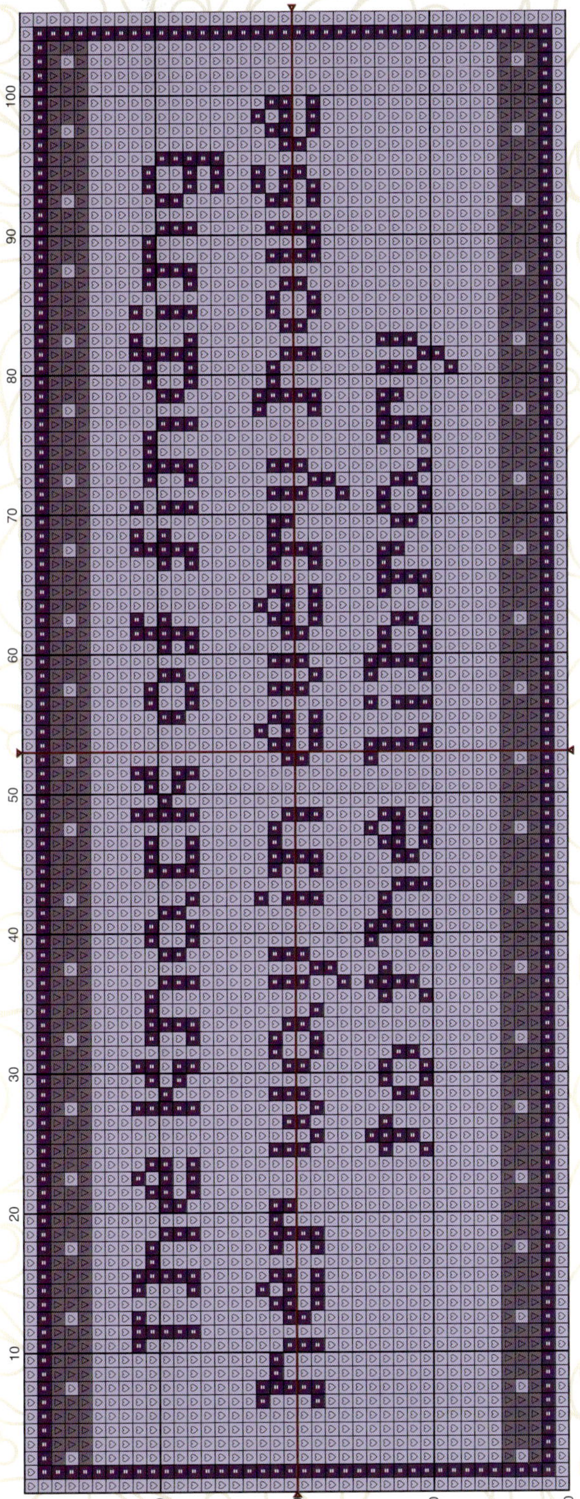

Sense and Sensibility

Symbol	Number	Color Name
♡	26	Lavender White
▽	28	Lavender Gray
=	550	Passionflower

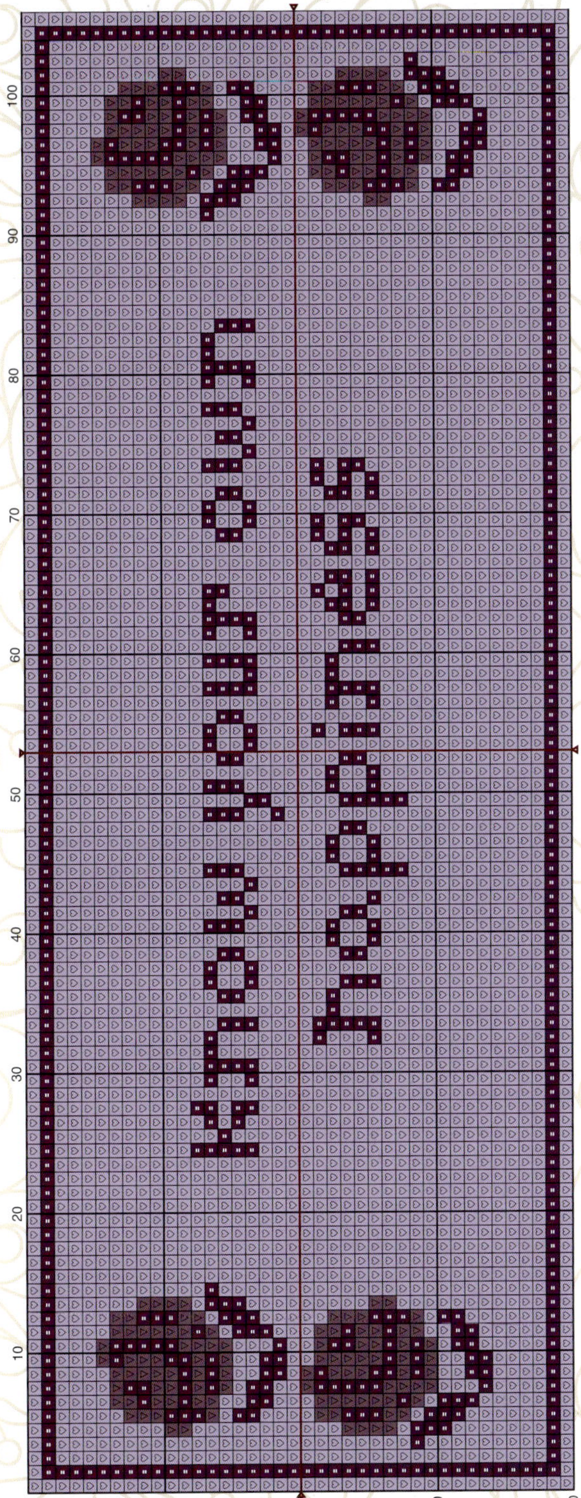

Pride and Prejudice

Pride and Prejudice

Symbol	Number	Color Name
☆	931	Blue Gray
♡	966	Pearlescent Soft Green
=	991	Frog

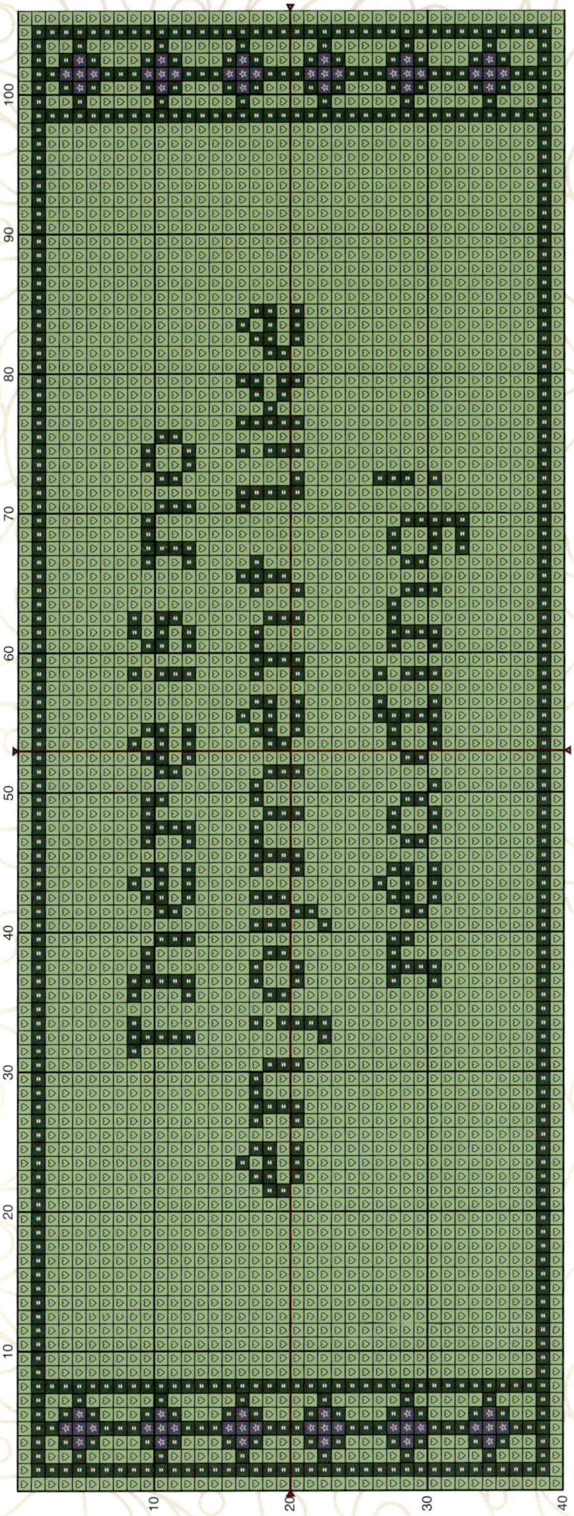

Pride and Prejudice

Symbol	Number	Color Name
▽	702	Spring Lawn
☆	931	Blue Gray
♡	966	Pearlescent Soft Green
=	991	Frog

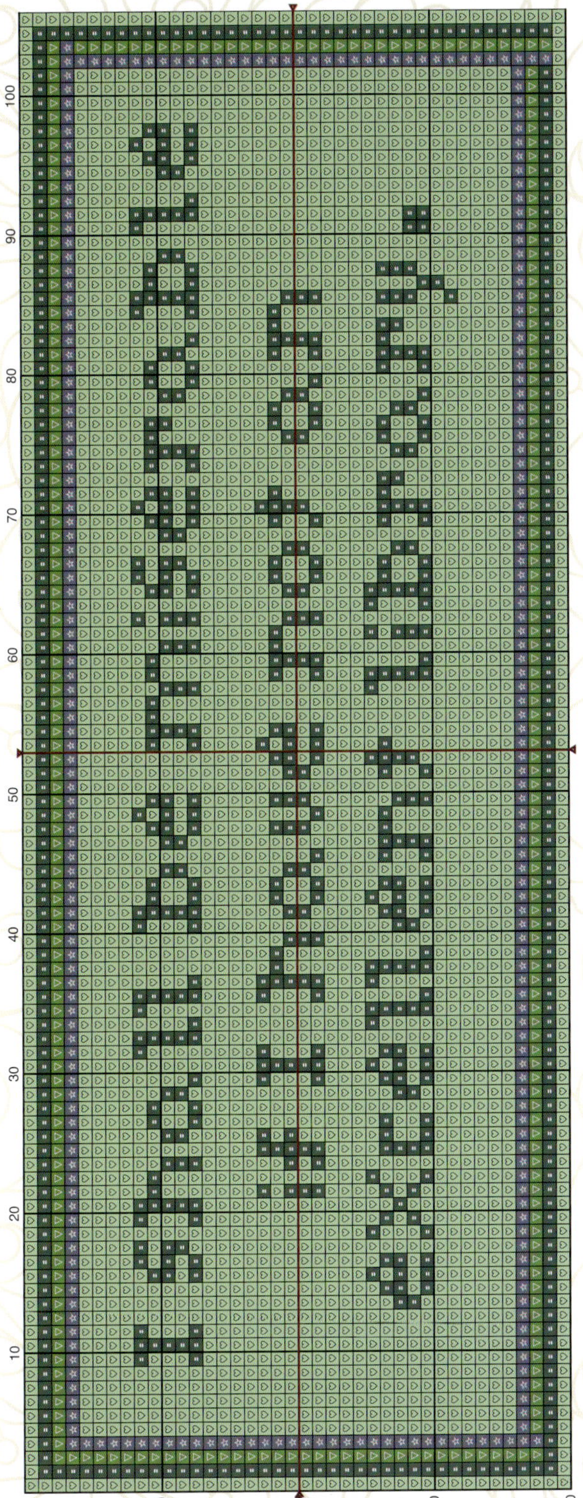

Pride and Prejudice

Symbol	Number	Color Name
♡	966	Pearlescent Soft Green
=	991	Frog

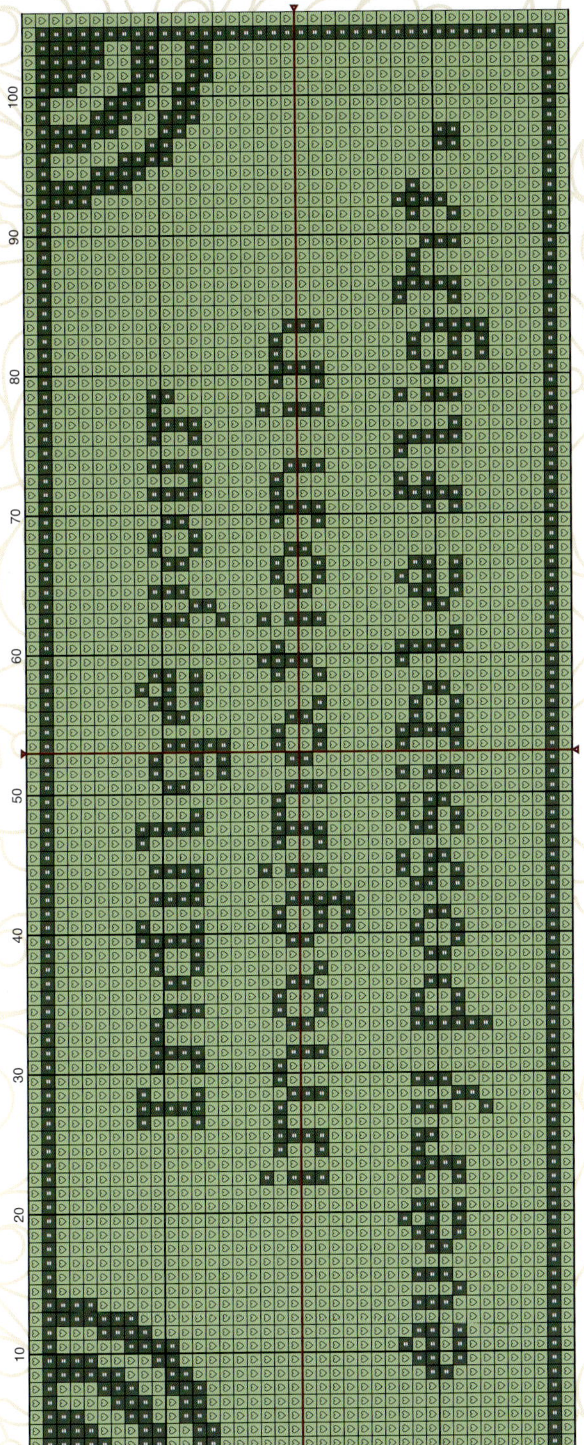

Pride and Prejudice

Symbol	Number	Color Name
▽	702	Spring Lawn
☆	931	Blue Gray
♡	966	Pearlescent Soft Green
=	991	Frog

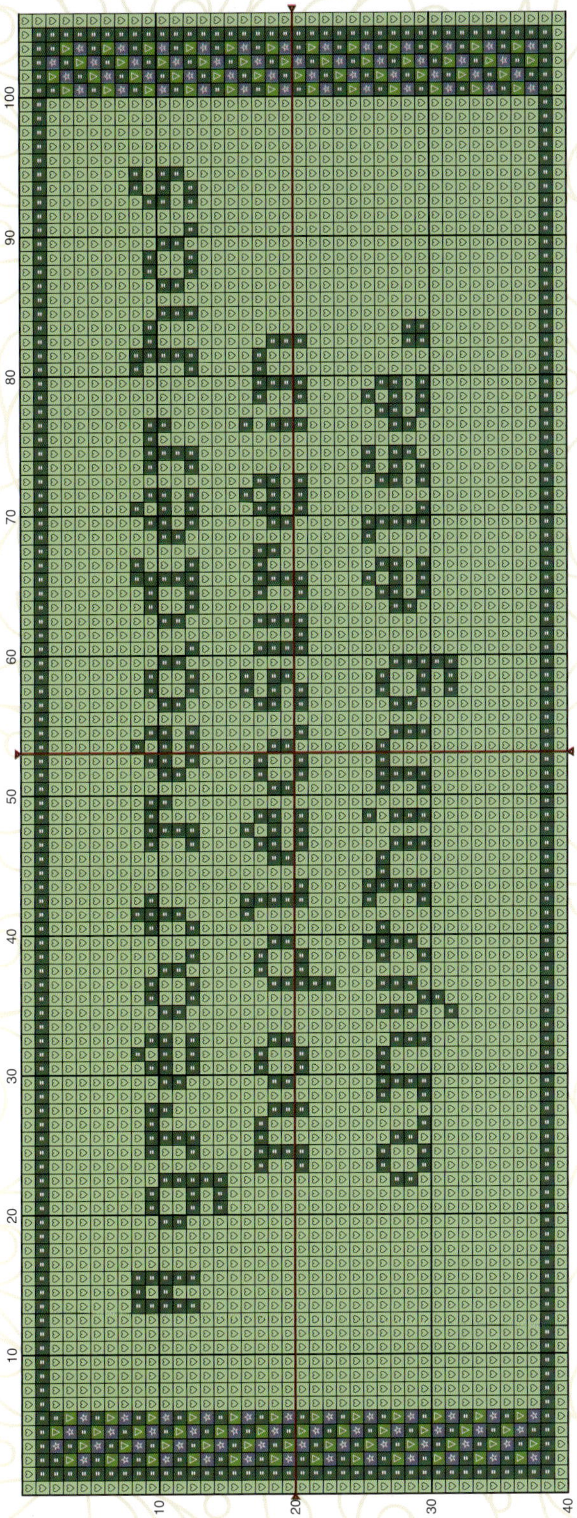

Pride and Prejudice

Symbol	Number	Color Name
▽	702	Spring Lawn
♡	966	Pearlescent Soft Green
=	991	Frog

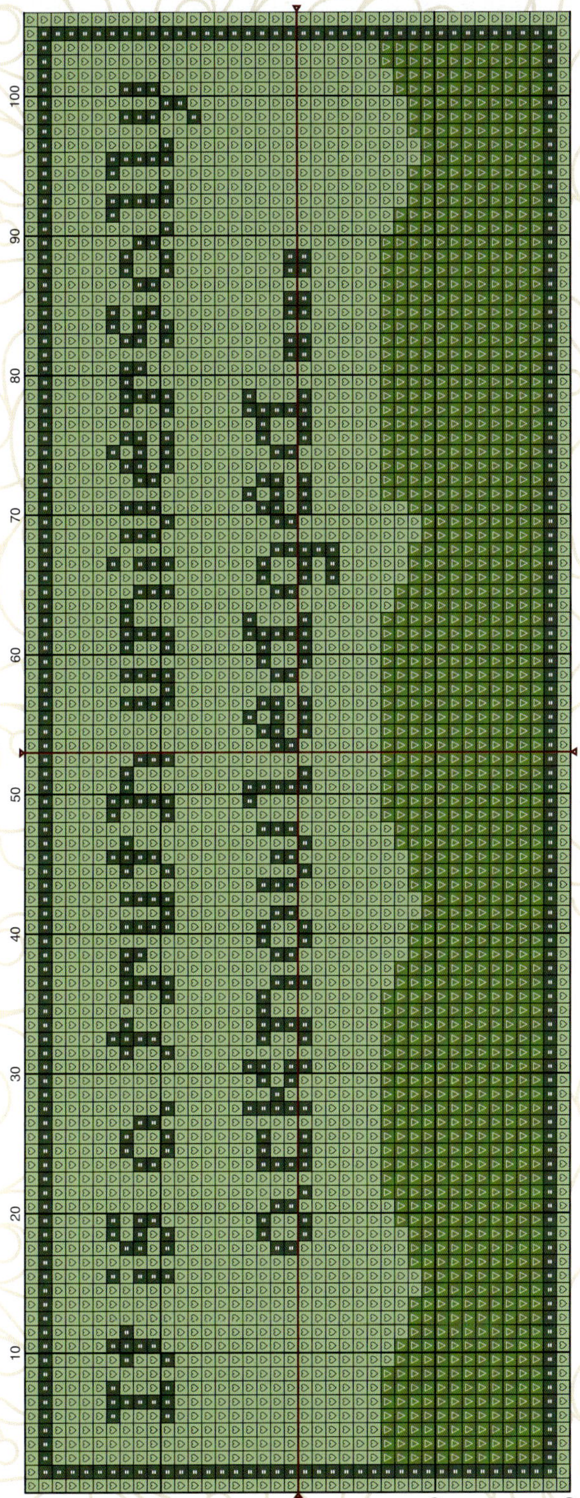

Northanger Abbey

Northanger Abbey

Symbol	Number	Color Name
=	01	Rain
♡	3799	Anthracite

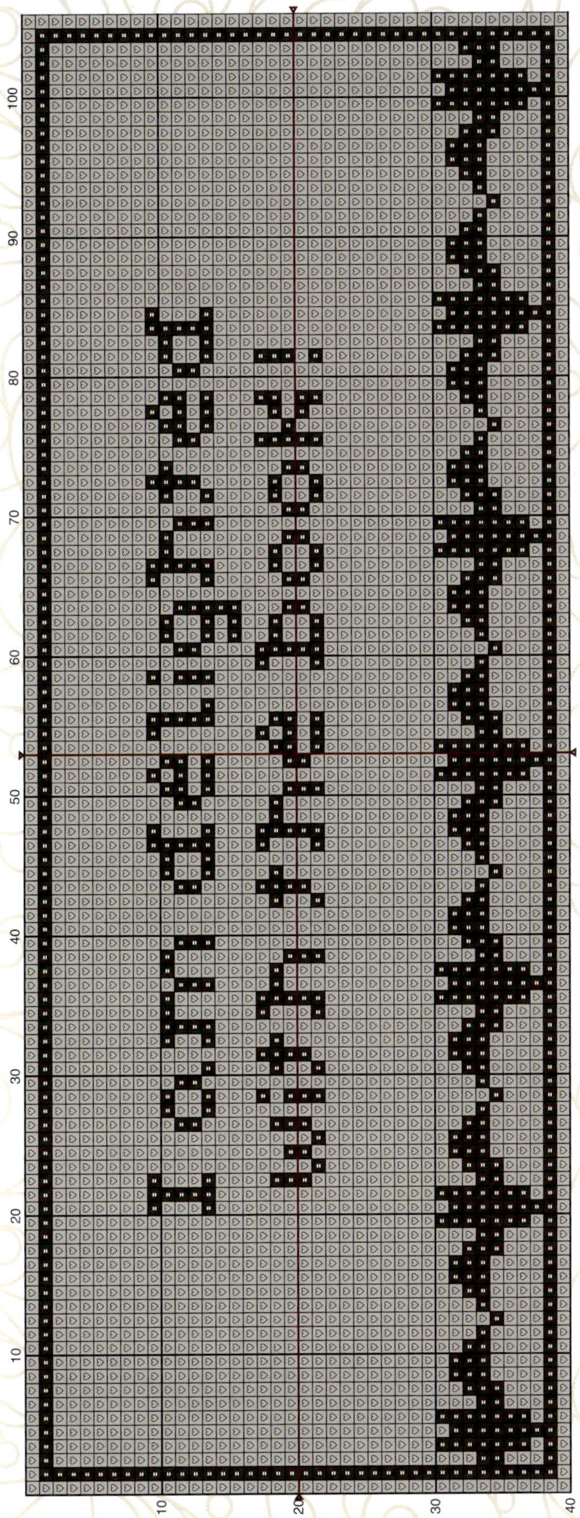

Northanger Abbey

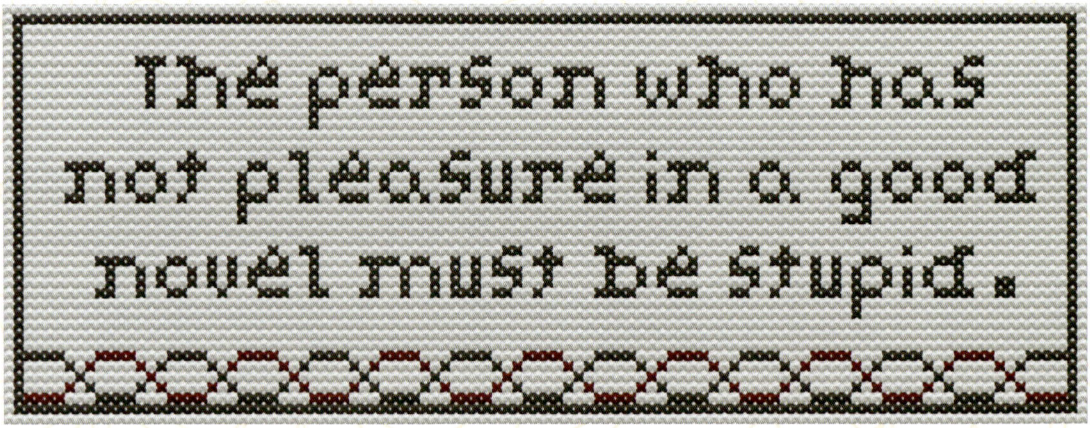

Symbol	Number	Color Name
=	01	Rain
☆	814	Vin Rouge
♡	3799	Anthracite

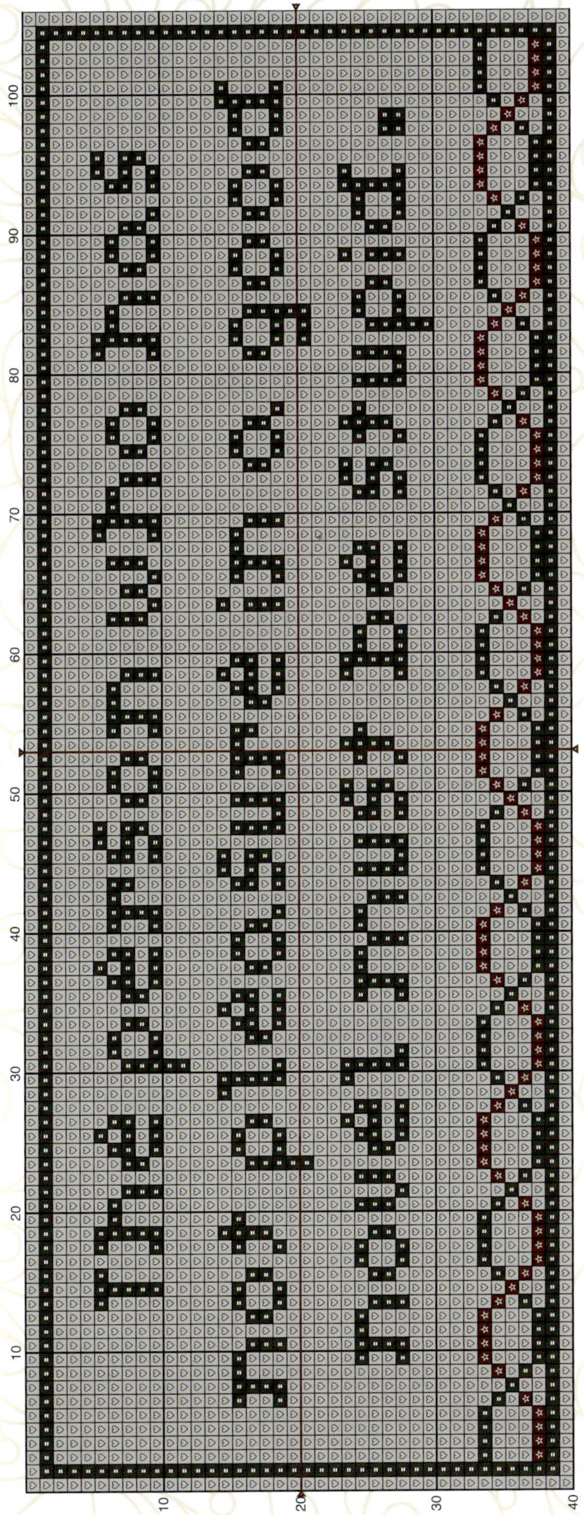

Northanger Abbey

Symbol	Number	Color Name
=	01	Rain
☆	814	Vin Rouge
♡	3799	Anthracite
▽	BLANC	Blanc

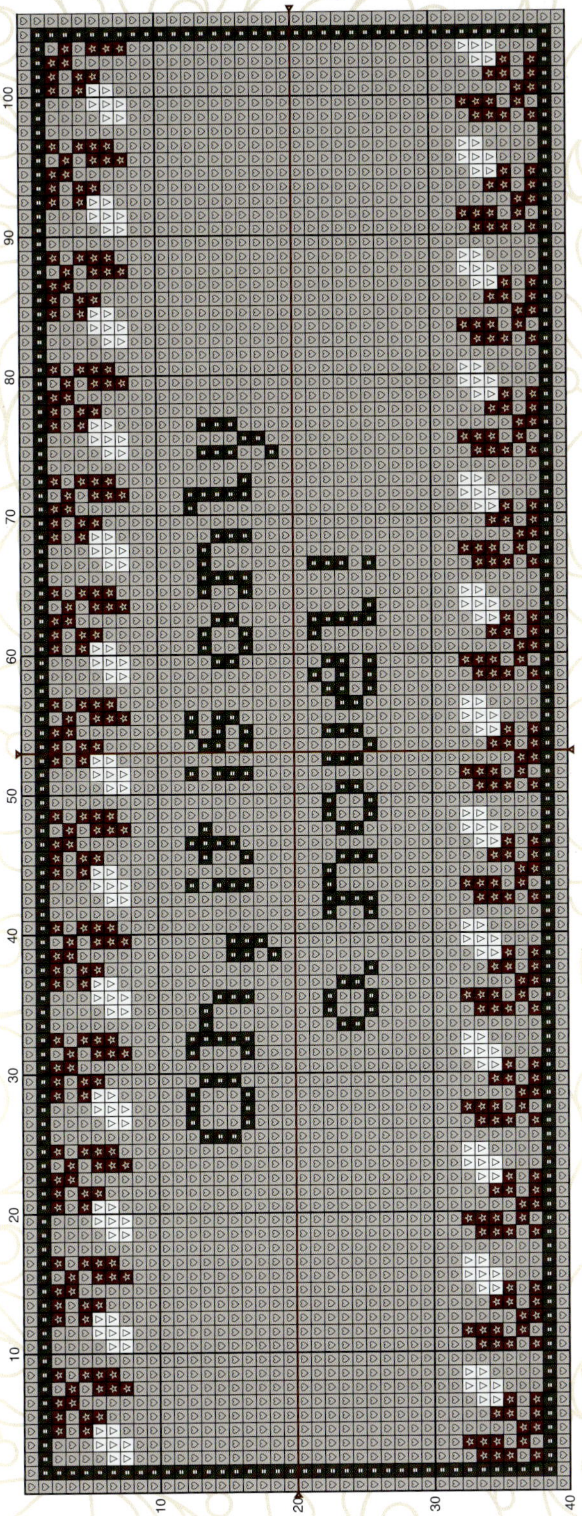

Northanger Abbey

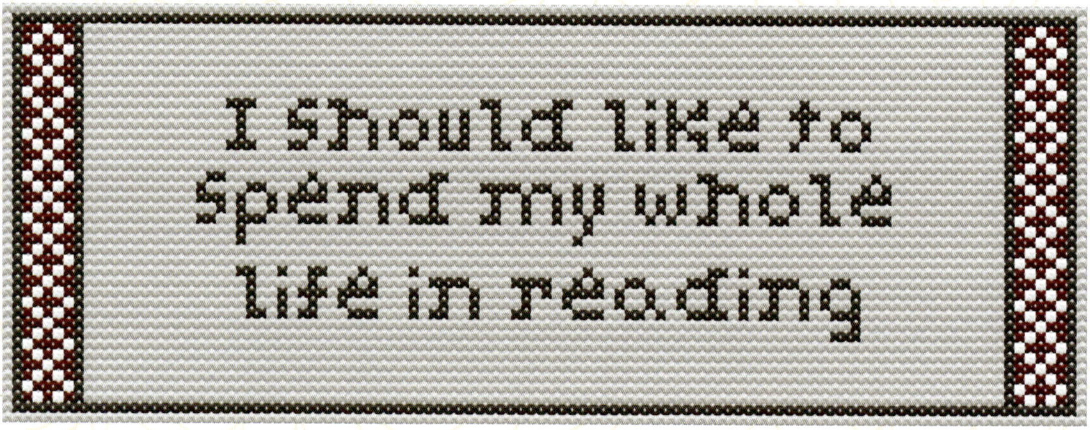

Symbol	Number	Color Name
=	01	Rain
☆	814	Vin Rouge
♡	3799	Anthracite
▽	BLANC	Blanc

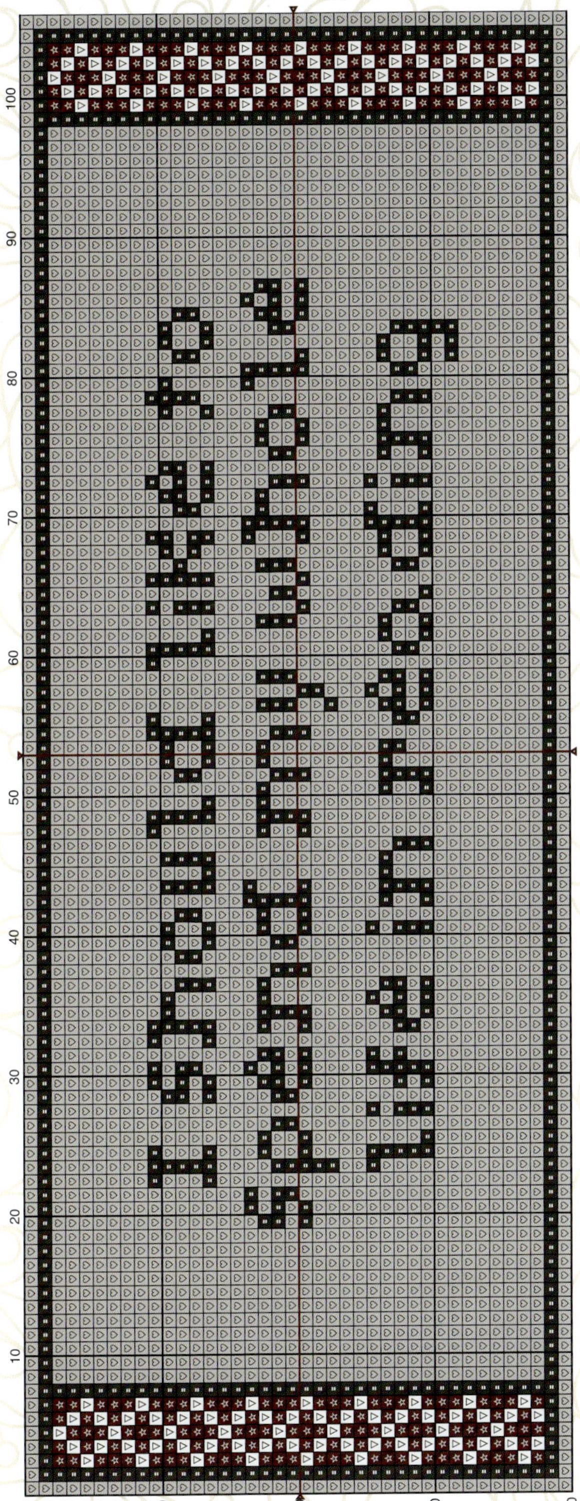

Northanger Abbey

Symbol	Number	Color Name
=	01	Rain
☆	814	Vin Rouge
♡	3799	Anthracite

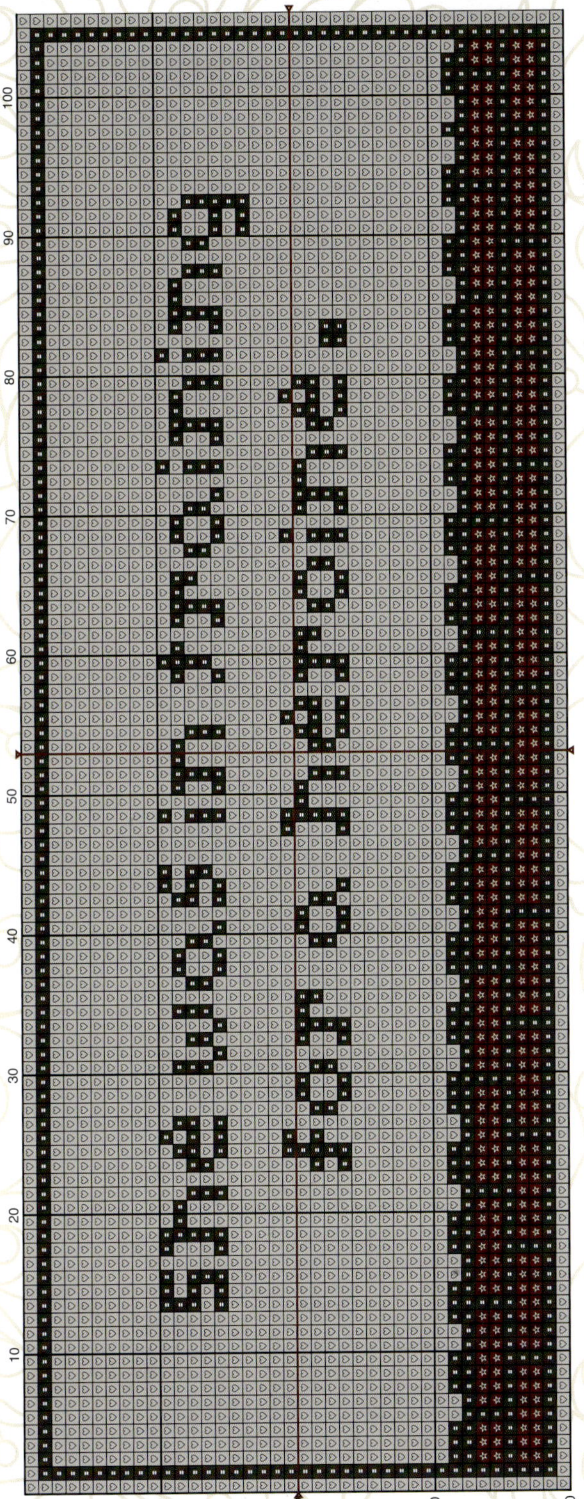

Mansfield Park

Mansfield Park

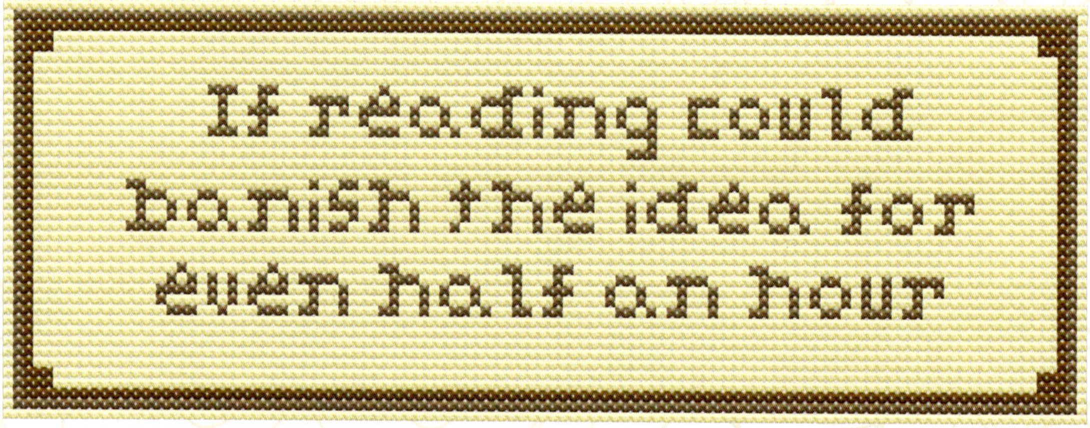

Symbol	Number	Color Name
▽	829	Star Anise
∘	840	Country Mouse
♡	3823	Moonshine

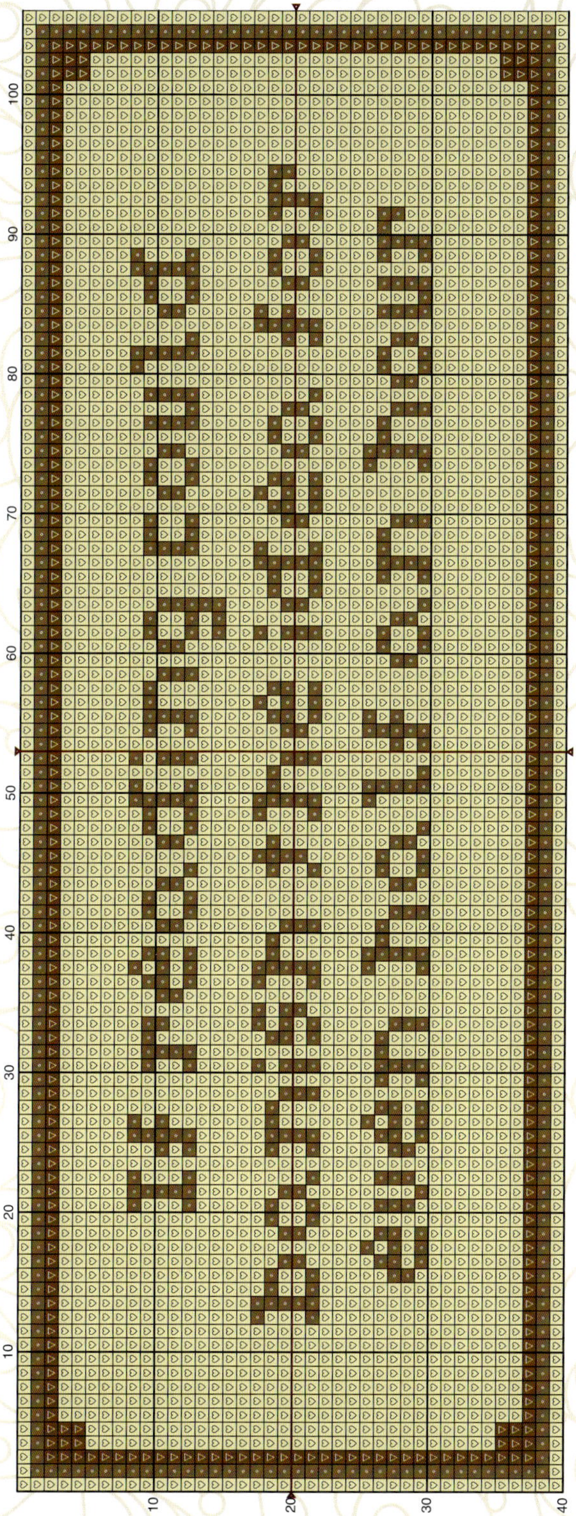

Mansfield Park

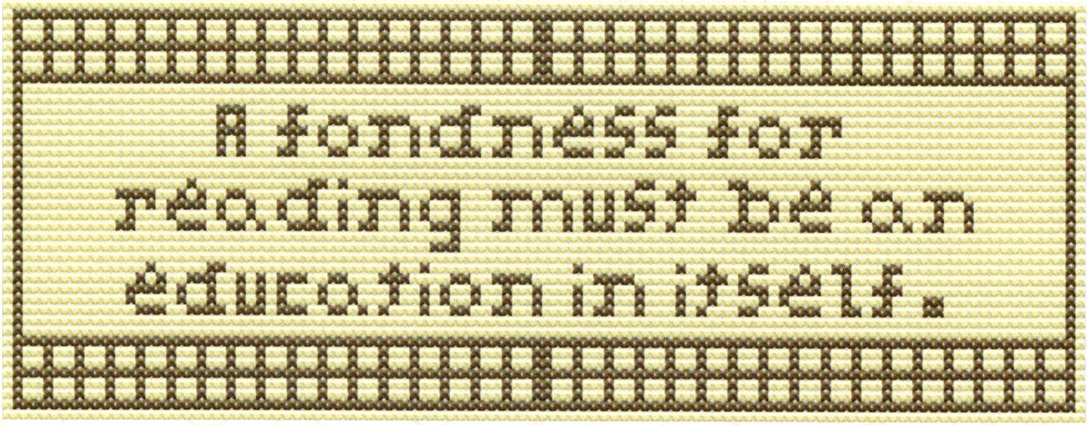

Symbol	Number	Color Name
∘	840	Country Mouse
♡	3823	Moonshine

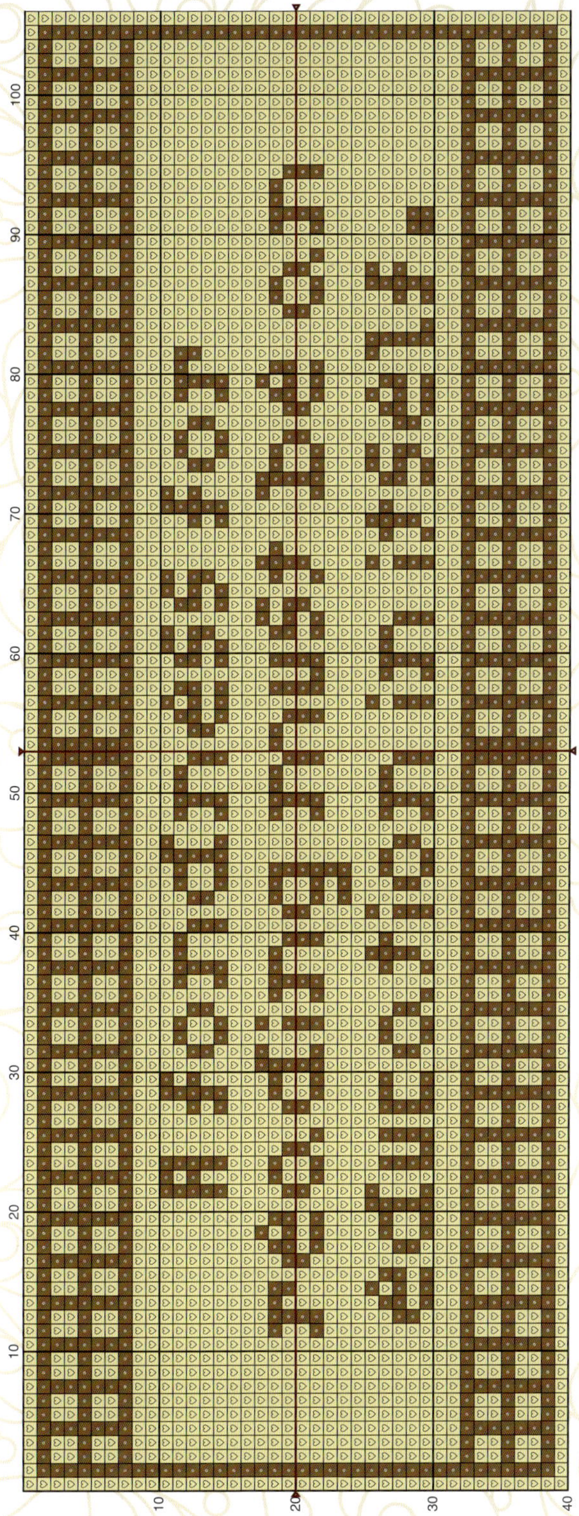

Mansfield Park

Symbol	Number	Color Name
▽	829	Star Anise
∘	840	Country Mouse
♡	3823	Moonshine

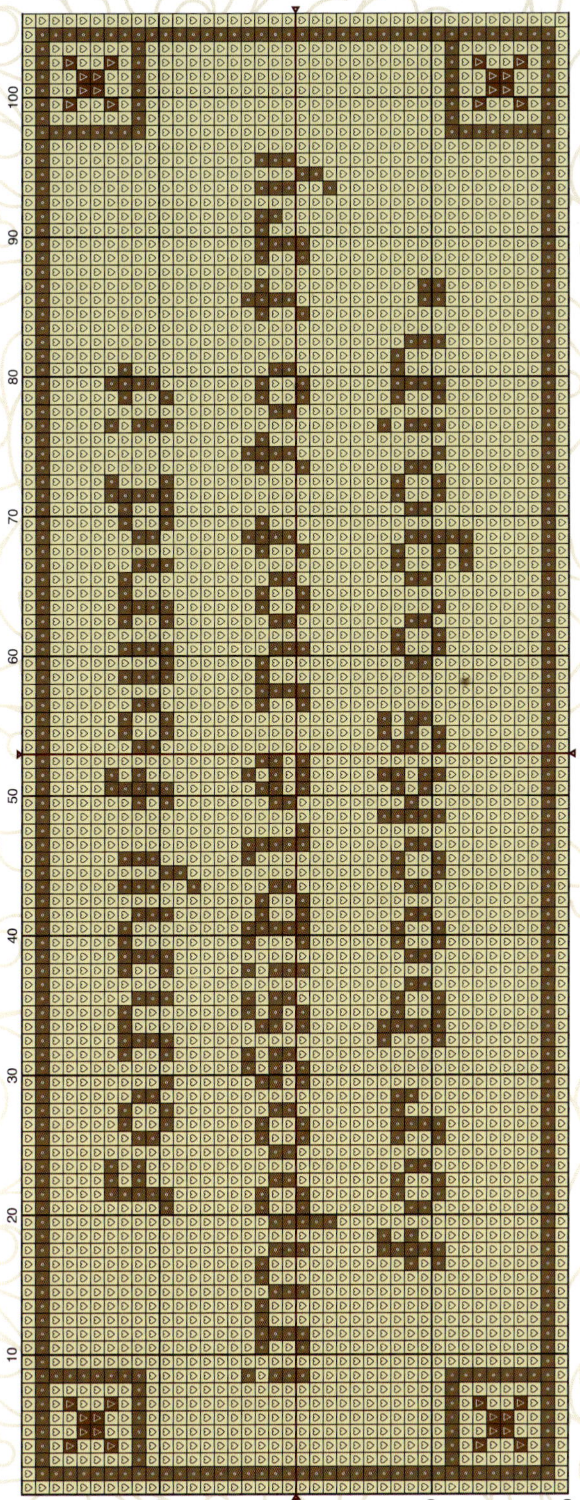

Mansfield Park

Symbol	Number	Color Name
∘	840	Country Mouse
♡	3823	Moonshine

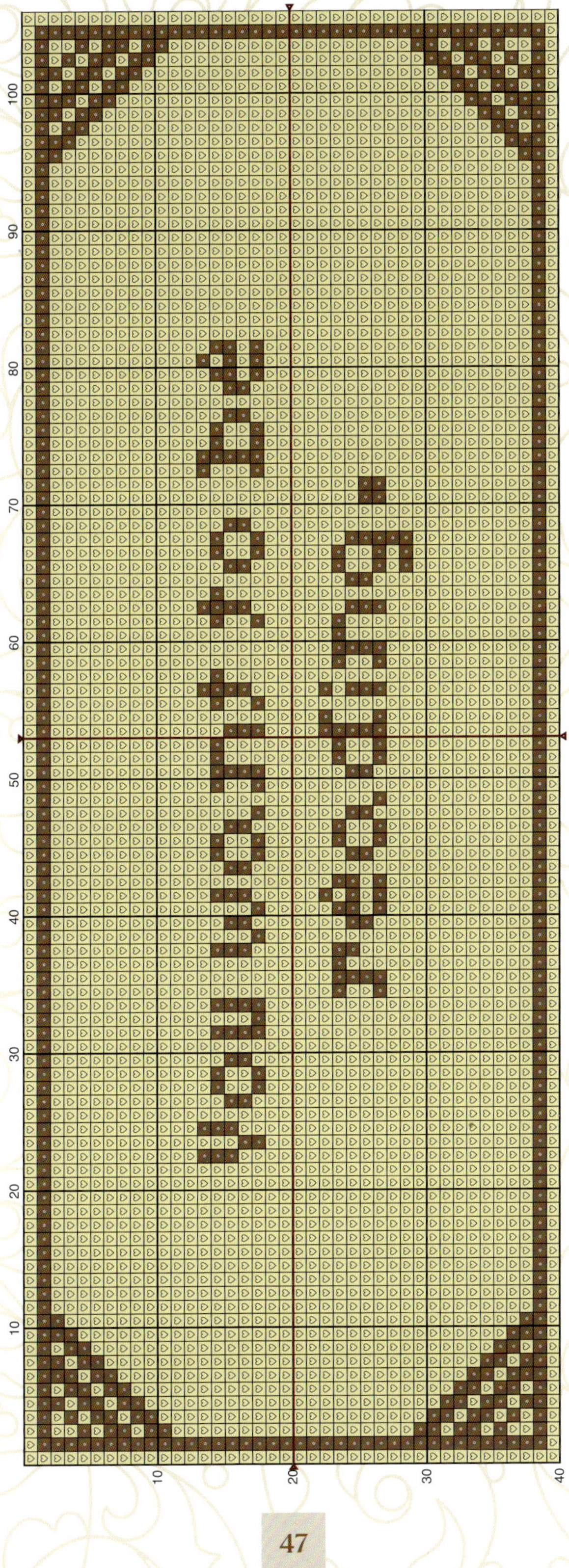

Mansfield Park

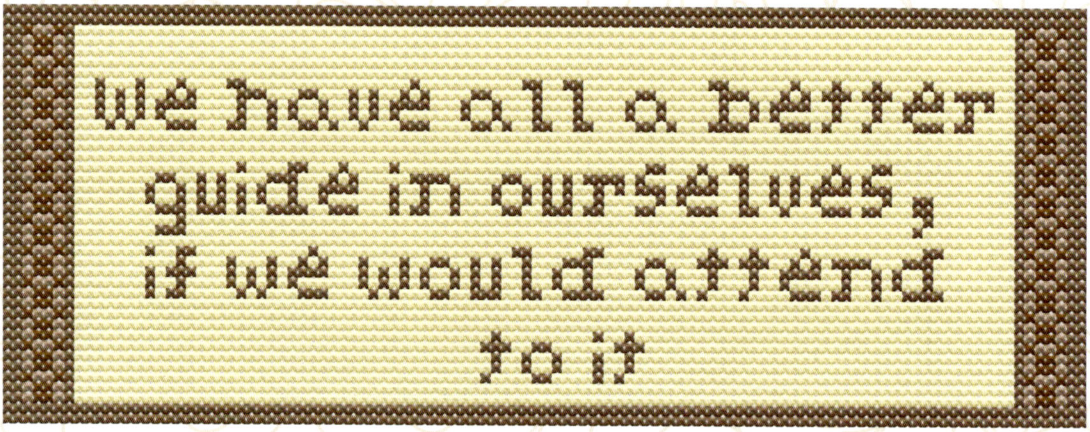

Symbol	Number	Color Name
▽	829	Star Anise
∘	840	Country Mouse
■	841	Suede
♡	3823	Moonshine

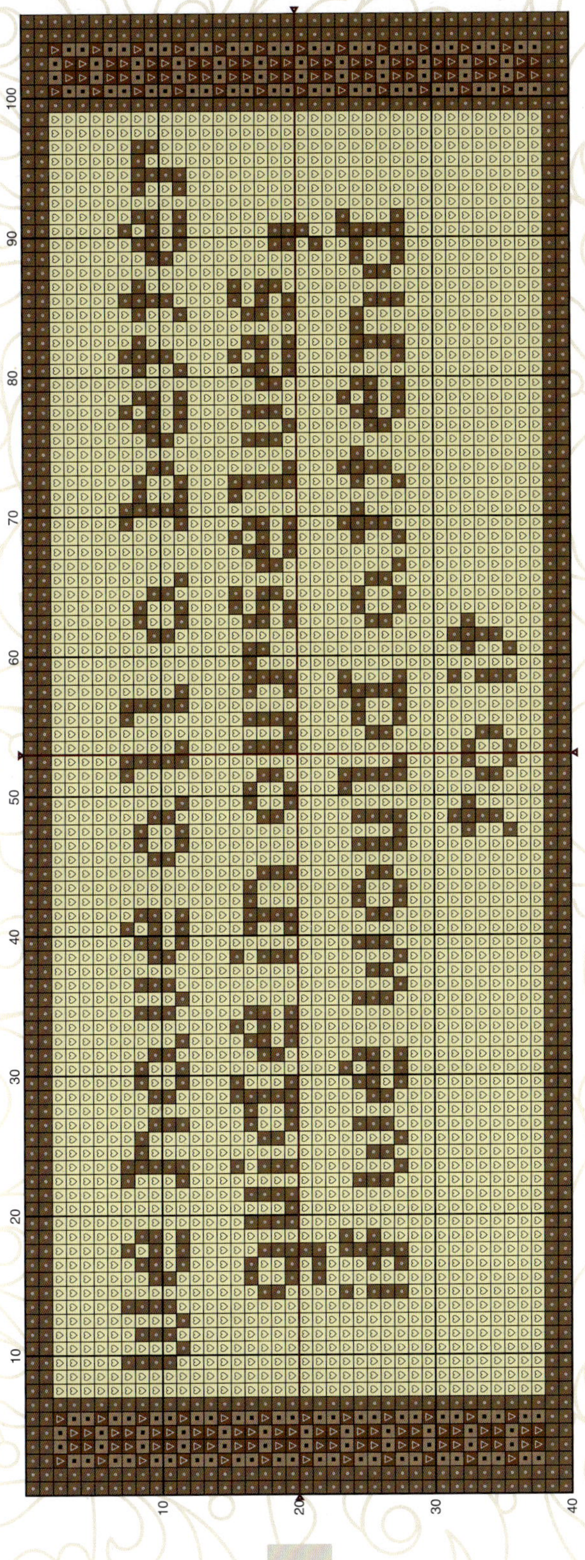

Emma

Emma

Symbol	Number	Color Name
	814	Vin Rouge
	963	Candy Pink
	3052	Silver Green
	3733	Pink Hollyhock

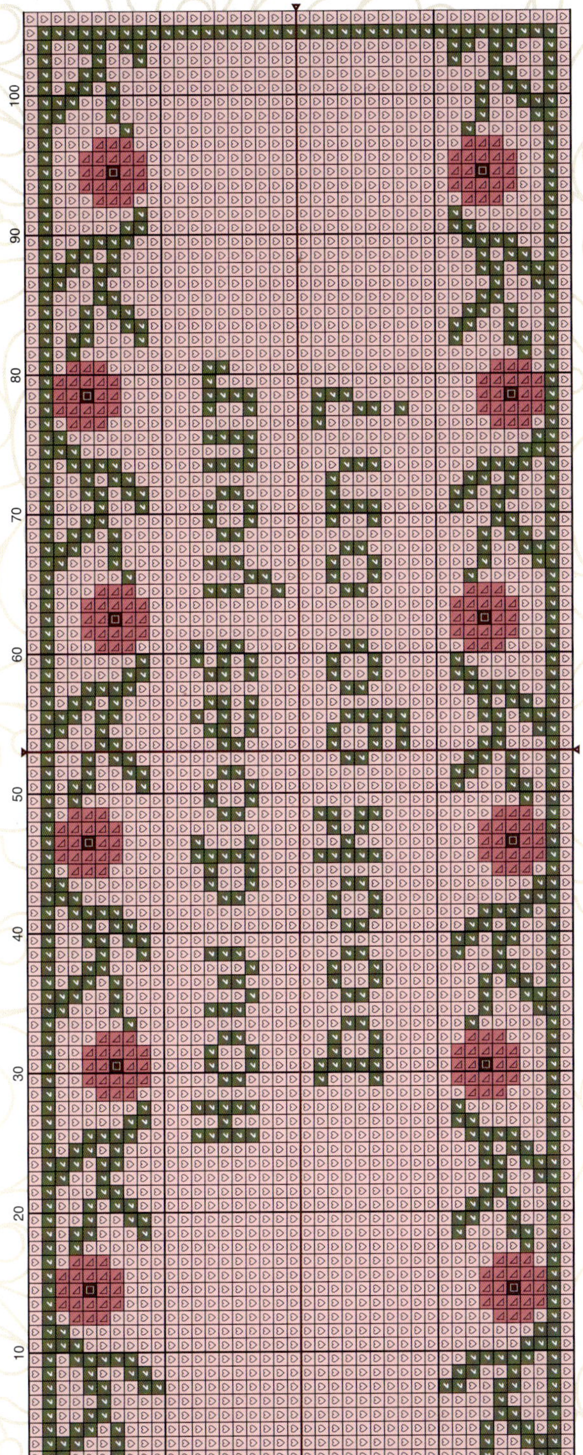

Emma

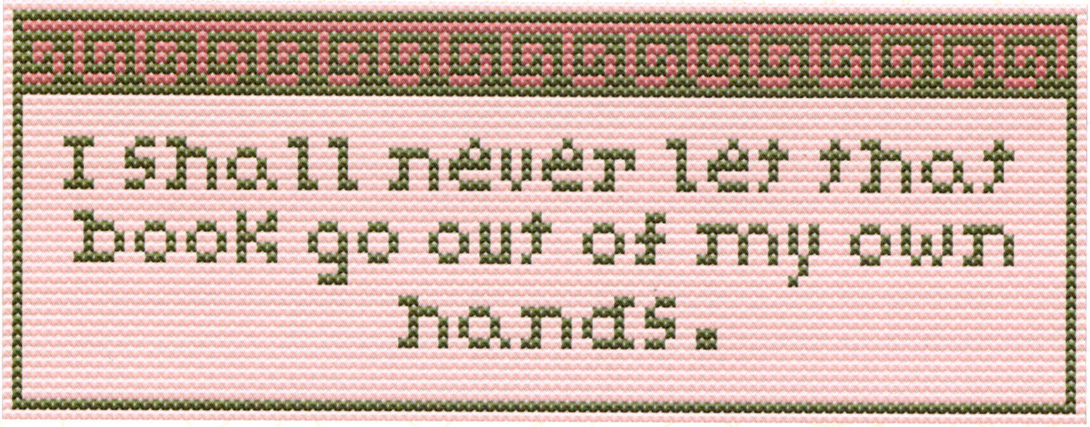

Symbol	Number	Color Name
♡	963	Candy Pink
∠	3052	Silver Green
◺	3733	Pink Hollyhock

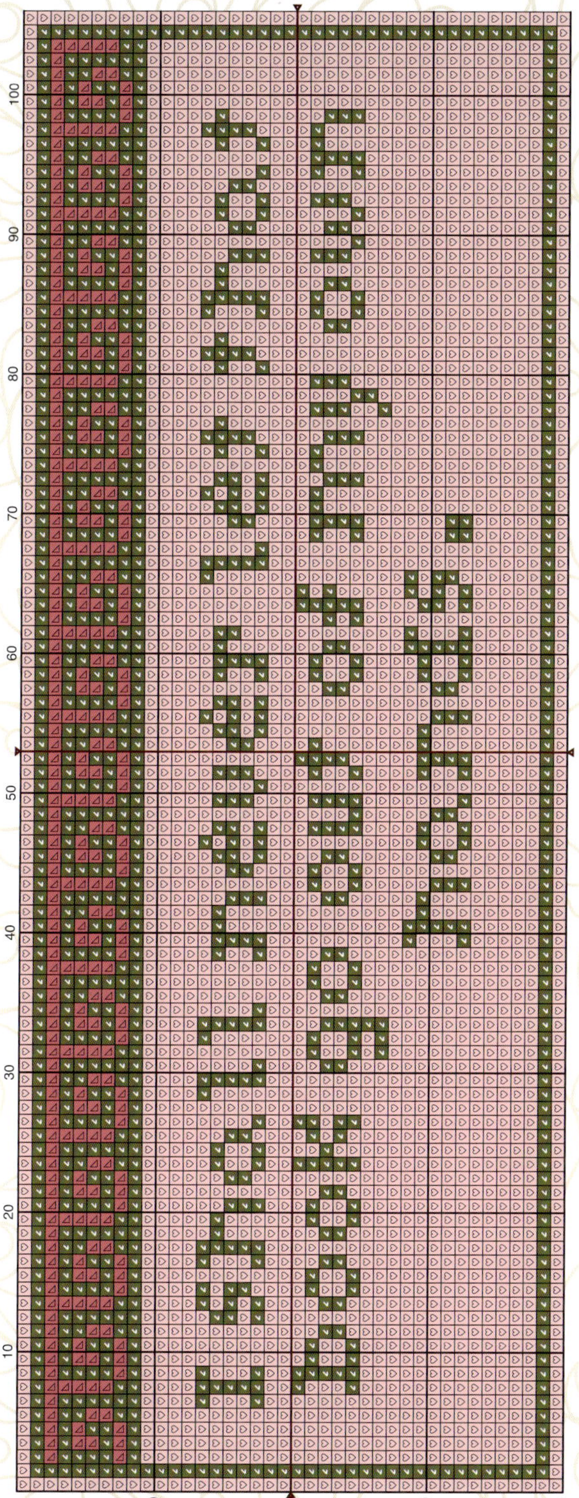

Emma

Symbol	Number	Color Name
♡	963	Candy Pink
∠	3052	Silver Green

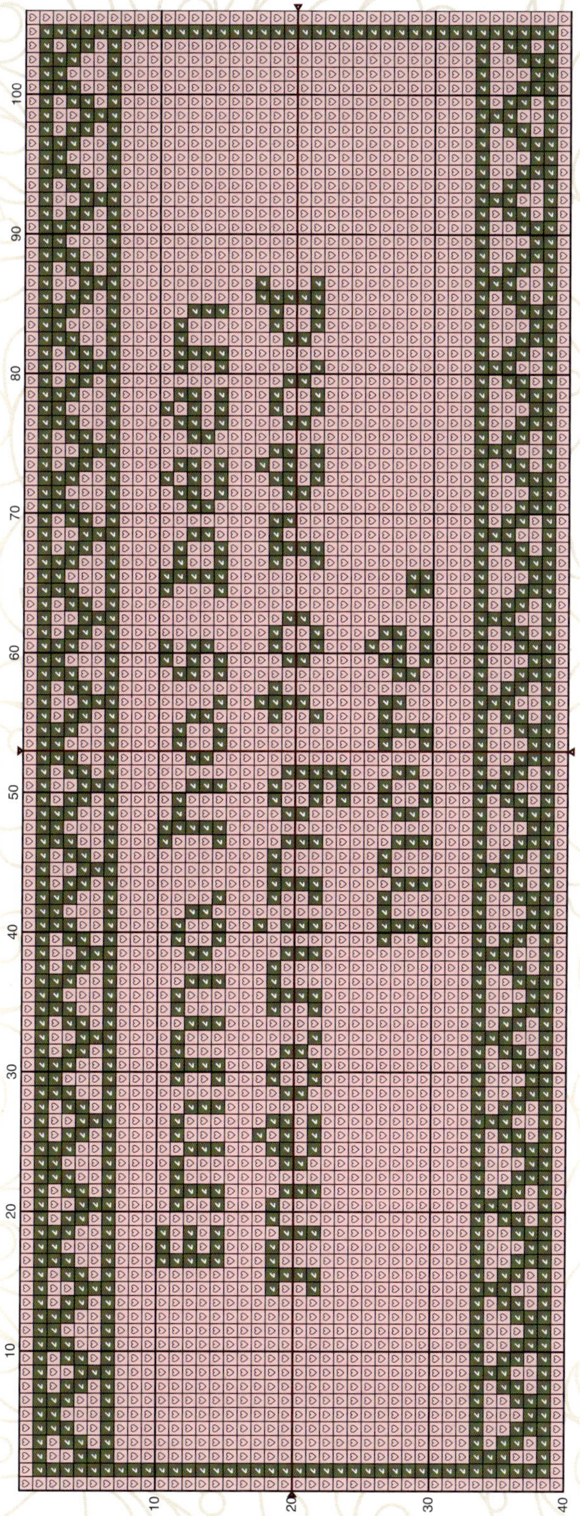

Emma

Symbol	Number	Color Name
♡	963	Candy Pink
∠	3052	Silver Green

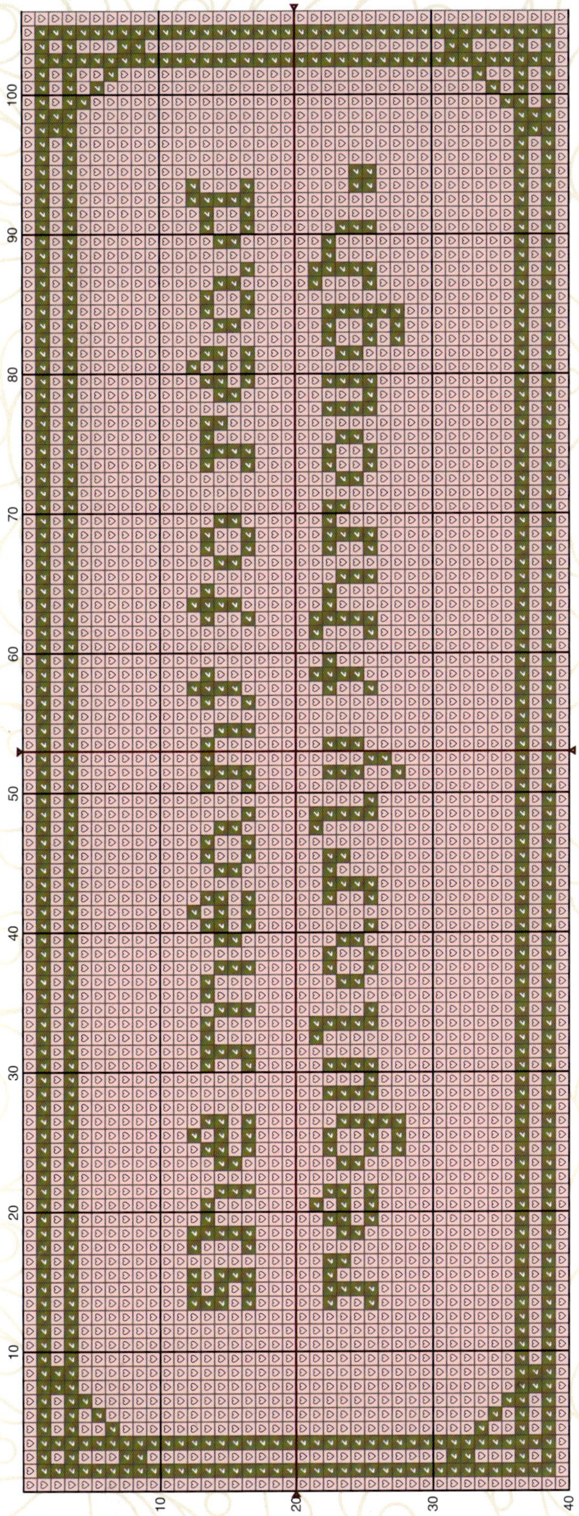
10
20
30
40
50
60
70
80
90
100
10
20
30
40

Emma

Symbol	Number	Color Name
♡	963	Candy Pink
∠	3052	Silver Green
◺	3733	Pink Hollyhock

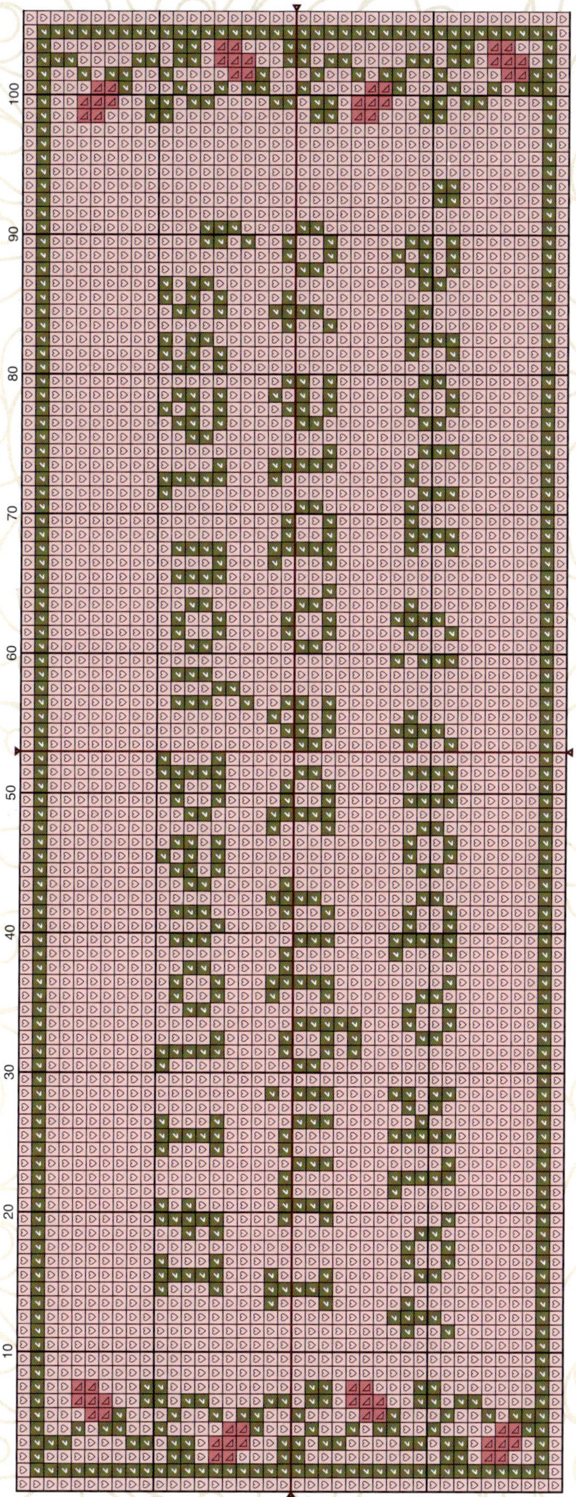
10
20
30
40
50
60
70
80
90
100
10
20
30
40

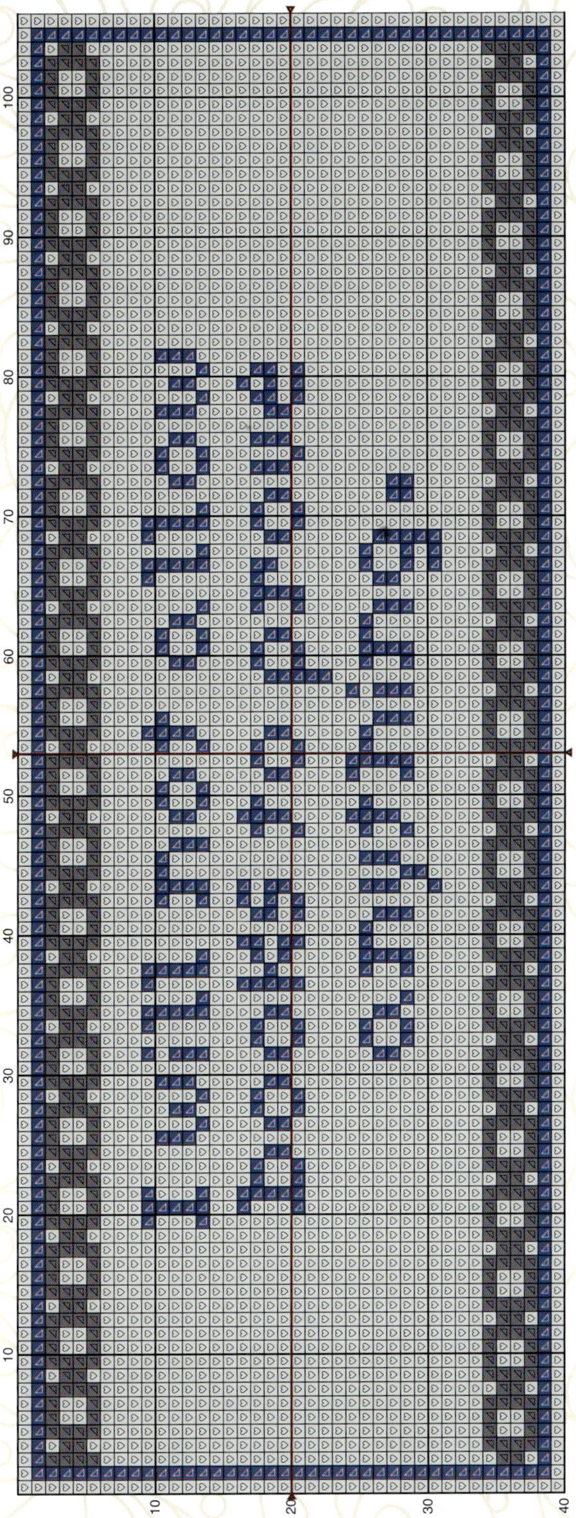
10
20
30
40
50
60
70
80
90
100
10
20
30
40

Persuasion

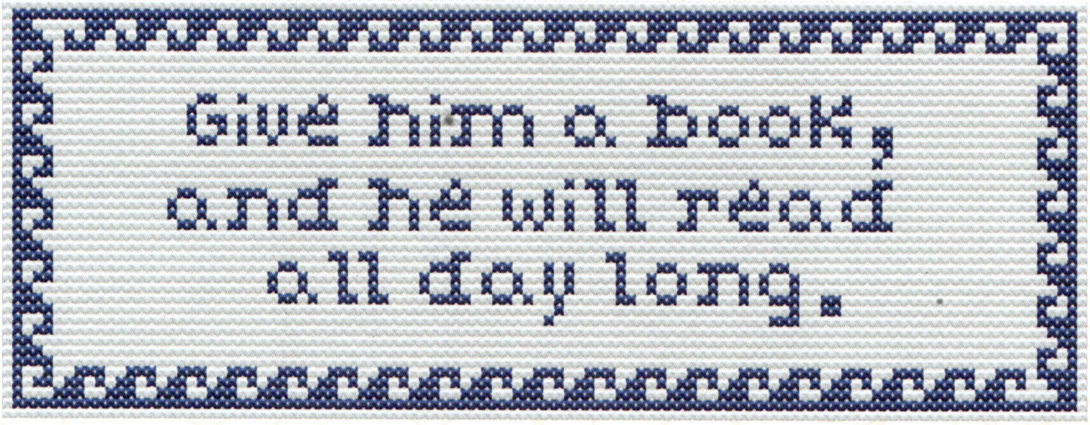

Symbol	Number	Color Name
♡	762	Pearl Gray
◺	3765	Blue Teal

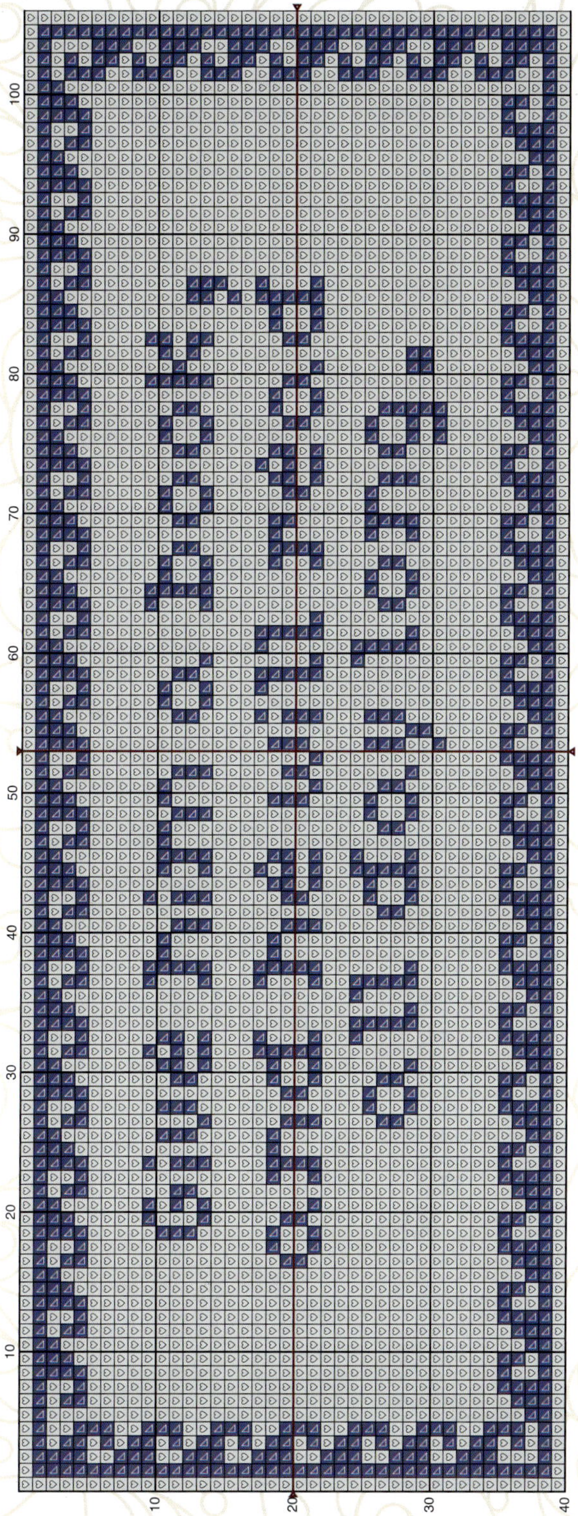

Persuasion

Symbol	Number	Color Name
♡	762	Pearl Gray
∘	840	Country Mouse
◺	3765	Blue Teal

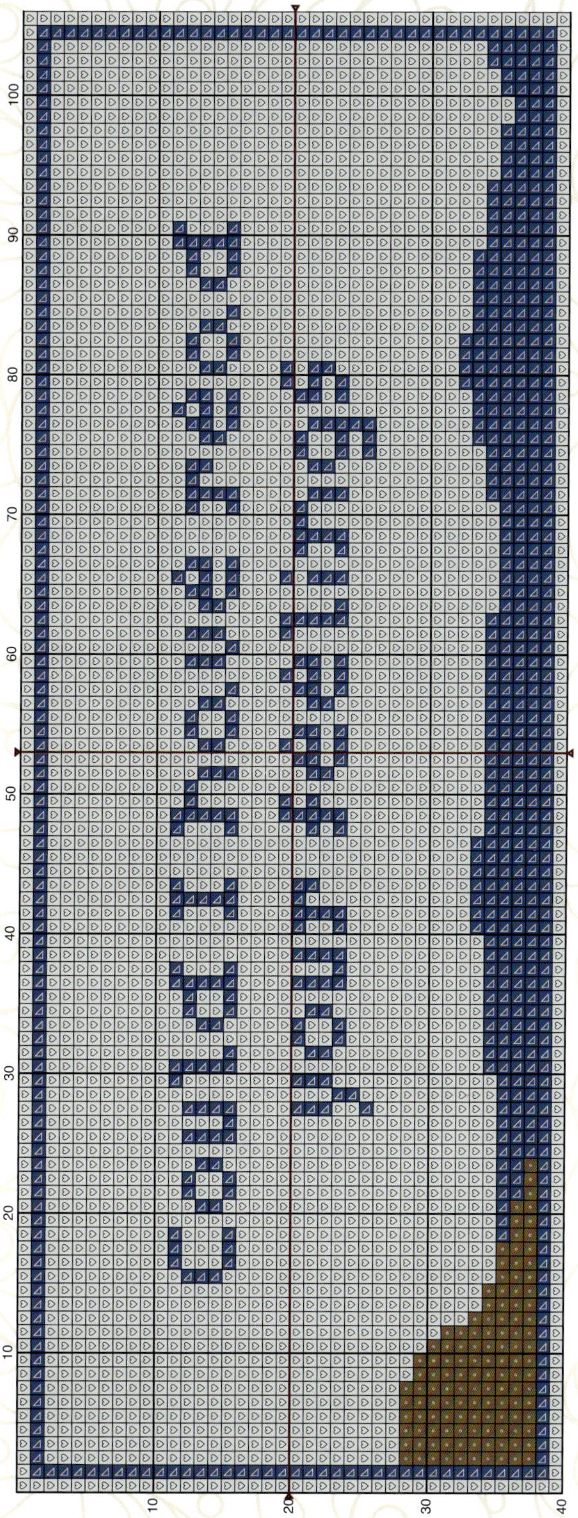
10
20
30
40
50
60
70
80
90
100
10
20
30
40

Persuasion

Symbol	Number	Color Name
♡	762	Pearl Gray
◺	3765	Blue Teal

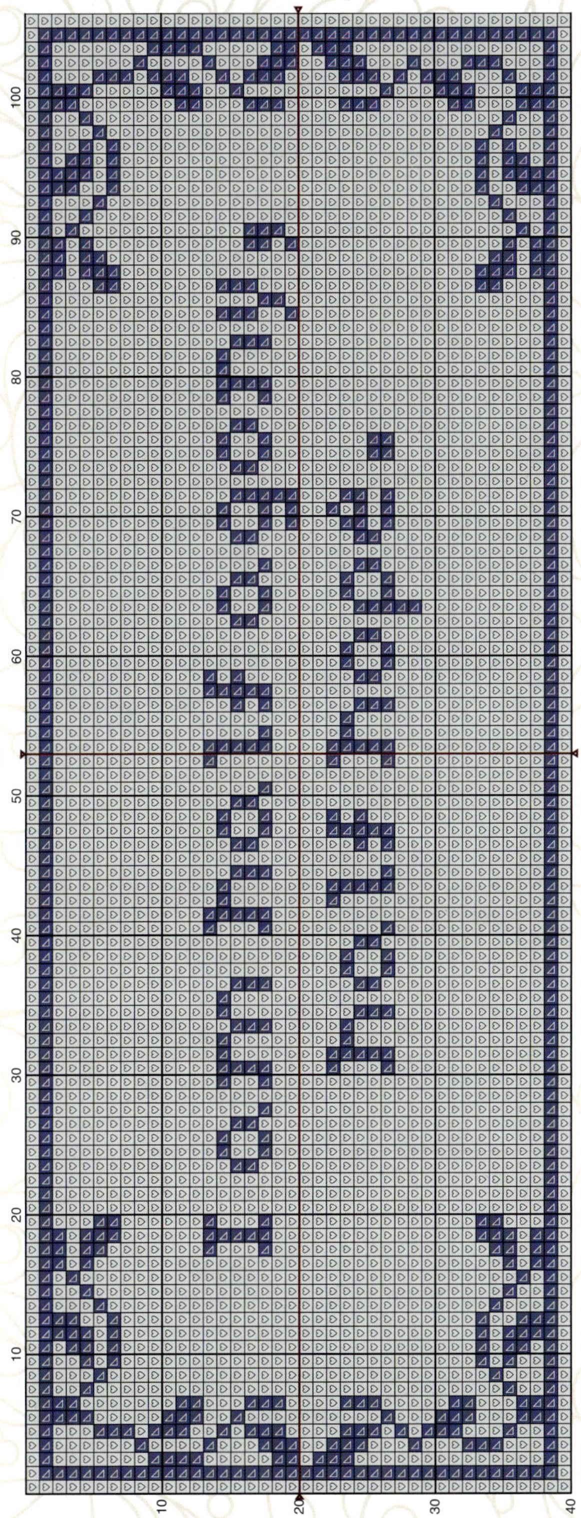
10
20
30
40
50
60
70
80
90
100
10
20
30
40

Persuasion

Persuasion

Symbol	Number	Color Name
♡	762	Pearl Gray
∘	840	Country Mouse
◺	3765	Blue Teal

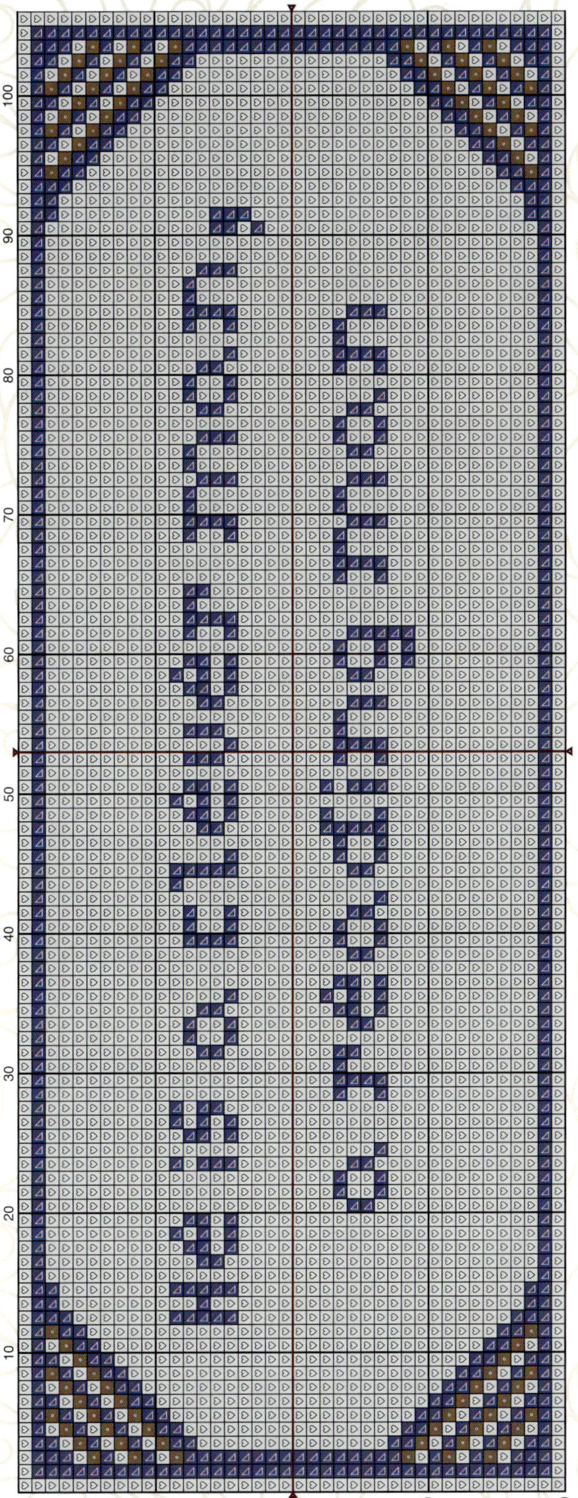

Persuasion

Symbol	Number	Color Name
◿	414	Lead
♡	762	Pearl Gray
◺	3765	Blue Teal